THE WRONG KIND OF BARK

WRITTEN BY
JULIA DONALDSON

ILLUSTRATED BY
GARRY PARSONS

For Hamish and Jeddah
J.D.

For Christopher and Emma
G.P.

Crabtree Publishing Company
www.crabtreebooks.com

PMB 16A, 350 Fifth Avenue,
Suite 3308,
New York, NY 10118

616 Welland Avenue,
St. Catharines, Ontario
Canada, L2M 5V6

Donaldson, Julia.
 The wrong kind of bark/ written by Julia Donaldson ; illustrated by Garry
Parsons.
 p. cm. -- (Red bananas)
 Summary: A daydreaming student misunderstands a nature study homework
assignment, with humorous results.
 ISBN-13: 978-0-7787-1073-8 (rlb) -- ISBN-10: 0-7787-1073-4 (rlb)
 ISBN-13: 978-0-7787-1089-9 (pbk) -- ISBN-10: 0-7787-1089-0 (pbk)
 [1. Schools--Fiction. 2. Nature study--Fiction.] I. Parsons, Garry, ill.
 II. Title. III. Series.

PZ7.D71499Wr 2005
[E]--dc22   2005001569 LC

Published by Crabtree Publishing in 2005
First published in 2004 by Egmont Books Ltd.
Text copyright © Julia Donaldson 2004
Illustrations © Garry Parsons 2004
The Author and Illustrator have asserted their moral rights.
Paperback ISBN 0-7787-1089-0
Reinforced Hardcover Binding ISBN 0-7787-1073-4

Contents

Red Bananas

Finlay and the Fish

Finlay sat next to the fish tank. He liked watching the fish. They were more interesting than the teacher.

There was a little bridge at the bottom of the fish tank. But the fish never swam under it. Or maybe they did when Finlay wasn't looking.

The big fish was swimming very close to the bridge now.

"Go on!" Finlay whispered. "Swim under it!"

The teacher was talking to the class. "Tomorrow, I want you all to bring in a flower for the nature table," she said. "It can be any kind of flower."

Finlay watched the big fish. It swam over the bridge.

"Finlay!" said the teacher. "What did I just say?"

"Any kind of flower," said Finlay.

"Yes," said the teacher. "And stop staring at the fish!"

Any kind of flower.

The Wrong Kind of Flower

"Did you all remember to bring in a flower?" asked the teacher the next day.

Most of the class had.

Me, Miss!

Sally Wong had
a marigold.

David Simmons
had a rose. A lot of
it had been eaten
by a green fly.

Ruth Goodchild
had a pansy. She
had some extra
flowers for the
teacher too.

I grew it myself.

The teacher filled a jar with water. She put it on the nature table. "Now, everyone put your flowers in here," she said.

Sally Wong put in the marigold.

David Simmons put in what was left of the rose.

Ruth Goodchild put in the pansy.

"Excuse me, Miss," she said. "Look what Finlay's doing."

The teacher looked at Finlay. He was pouring some white stuff out of a bag into the water.

"What are you doing, Finlay?" asked the teacher.

"Putting my flour in the water, like you said, Miss," said Finlay.

"That's the wrong kind of flour," said the
teacher. She had to change the water.

Later on, Finlay was watching the fish again. The little one was swimming very close to the bridge.

"Go on!" whispered Finlay. "Swim under it!"

The teacher was talking to the class. "Tomorrow, I want you all to bring in a nut for the nature table," she said. "It can be any kind of nut."

Finlay watched the little fish. It swam around the bridge.

"Finlay!" said the teacher. "What did I just say?"

"Any kind of nut," said Finlay.

"Yes," said the teacher. "And stop staring at the fish!"

The Wrong Kind of Nut

"Did you all remember to bring in a nut?" asked the teacher the next day.

Most of the class had.

Sally Wong had
a walnut.

David Simmons
had a chestnut. It
was a bit broken.

Ruth Goodchild
had a coconut.
She had a package
of peanuts for the
teacher too.

Mine's the biggest!

"Now, put them all on the nature table," said the teacher.

Sally Wong put down the walnut.

David Simmons put down the broken chestnut.

Miss! Miss!

Ruth Goodchild put down the coconut.

"Excuse me, Miss," she said. "Finlay's putting some metal things on the table. That's not what you said, Miss, is it?"

"What are those, Finlay?" said the teacher.

"They're nuts, like you said, Miss," said Finlay. "My dad was screwing some into some shelves and he let me have these ones."

"That's the wrong kind of nut," said the teacher.

She moved Finlay to a different table. "Now you can stop staring at the fish," she said.

Try and concentrate, Finlay.

"Okay," said the teacher. "It's time to practice our play."

The class was doing a play about nature. Some children had made masks.

Sally Wong had a daisy mask.

Finlay had a tomato mask.

David Simmons had a yellow mask. He was being the sun. He had cut one eye bigger than the other, but the teacher said it didn't matter.

Hey, Tomato face!

Some children were being raindrops. They had long paper ribbons tied to their arms. The ribbons were supposed to be the rain.

Ruth Goodchild was Mother Nature. She had a wand and was allowed to boss everybody around.

The children practiced the play in the hall. Then they came back to the classroom.

Finlay's new table was by the window. There was some scaffolding up outside. Some builders were going to do some work on the school roof. They were sitting on the scaffolding eating their lunch. One of them had dropped a bit of his sandwich. A bird was hopping towards it.

"Go on," whispered Finlay. "Get it!"

The teacher was talking to the class.
"I want you all to bring in part of a tree for the nature table," she said. "It can be a twig, or a leaf, or a little bit of bark."

Finlay watched the bird. It flew away.

"Finlay!" said the teacher. "What did I just say?"

"Bring in bark," said Finlay.

"Yes," said the teacher. "And stop staring out of the window."

The Wrong Kind of Bark

The teacher came into the classroom the next day.

There were a lot of children around Finlay's desk.

Miss! Miss!

"Excuse me, Miss," said Ruth Goodchild. "Finlay's got a dog. That's not what you said, Miss, is it?"

Finlay had a small puppy in his arms.

"Finlay, you can't bring pets to school," said the teacher.

"But you said to bring in a bark, Miss," said Finlay. The puppy barked loudly.

"That's the wrong kind of bark," said the teacher.

She phoned Finlay's home to see if his mom or dad could come for the puppy. But no one was home.

The teacher went back into the classroom.

The puppy was standing on the nature table. He was barking at the builders.

The jar of flowers was on its side. Most of the nuts were on the floor.

"Take him off the table, Finlay," said the teacher. She cleaned up the mess.

The puppy
went on and on
barking at the
builders. Finlay
put his jacket
under the
nature table.

"What are
you doing now,
Finlay?" asked
the teacher.

"I'm making
a bed for the
puppy," said
Finlay. The
puppy lay down
on the jacket.
He stopped
barking.

"Now it's time to do the play for the rest of the school," said the teacher.

The children put on their masks.

Sally Wong put on her daisy mask.

It's hot in here.

David Simmons put on his sun mask.

Finlay put on his tomato mask.

How do I tie this?

The puppy started to bark again. He barked and barked at the tomato mask.

"He doesn't like the tomato mask," said Finlay. "He thinks it's attacking me."

"Take the mask off," said the teacher. "You can put it on when we're down in the hall."

Finlay took off the tomato mask. The puppy growled. He grabbed the mask in his mouth and tore it up.

Stop it!

The teacher was very angry. "I'll have to tie him up," she said. She found some string. She tied one end of it to the puppy's collar. Then she tied the other end around a leg of Finlay's desk.

Finlay had to make a new tomato mask. There wasn't time for the paint to dry.

The teacher put the paint can up on a shelf. Then they went down to the hall to perform the play for the rest of the school.

The puppy was left alone in the classroom.

The builders were banging on the roof. The puppy barked at them. The builders kept on banging. The shelves on the wall started to shake. They shook and shook. The can of red paint jumped on the shelf. It fell on its side. The red paint started to run out of it . . .

Tomato Trouble

Down in the hall the children were doing their play. The children being flowers and fruit were curled up on the stage.

Ruth Goodchild was sitting in a chair
with tinsel tied on it. It was her throne.
"Pitter patter raindrops," she said. She waved
her wand.

The children being raindrops ran on to the
stage. They shook the ribbons on their arms.
They were supposed to be watering the
flowers and fruit.

I'm a
star!

David Simmons came on to the stage in his
sun mask. He stood stiffly over the plants.
From far away came a barking sound.
"Grow, plants, grow," said Ruth.

Did you hear that?

The children being flowers and fruit began to uncurl. Finlay uncurled. The red paint from his tomato mask dripped down his sweater.

Grow, plants, grow.

The barking grew louder and louder.

"Grow taller," said Ruth.

The flowers and fruit grew. Most of them grew slowly.

But the tomato shot up. It was still dripping red paint. The tomato jumped off the stage. It ran through the hall and up the stairs.

Ruth Goodchild looked angry.

The Right Kind of Bark

The teacher went out of the hall. Quietly, she followed the tomato up the stairs.

Finlay went into the classroom. The teacher followed him.

What's going on?

The puppy had stopped barking at the
builders. He was barking at the fish tank.
He was barking and barking and barking.

On the shelf the can of red paint lay on its side. Red paint was running out of it. A few drops had dripped into the fish tank.

"Quick!" said the teacher. "Bring me a jar of water, Finlay." She took the paint can off the shelf and put it on her desk.

There was a net next to the fish tank. The teacher fished the big fish out of the tank.

Finlay and the puppy watched. The puppy had stopped barking.

The teacher tried to fish out the little fish. But it was a very fast swimmer. It kept swimming away.

"Yes!" said Finlay. The little fish was swimming under the bridge!

The teacher held the net at the other side of the bridge and the little fish swam into it.

He did it!

The teacher took the fish into the classroom next door. They had a fish tank too. She put the fish in it.

"Now we'll have to change the water in our tank," she said. "We can't let the fish swallow red paint."

Later on, the other children came back to the classroom.

Ruth Goodchild still looked angry.

"I'm sorry I missed the end of the play," said the teacher. "But in a way I'm glad. If all the paint had gone into the water, the fish could have died. It's a good thing that Finlay's puppy warned us."

Finlay cuddled his puppy.

"Maybe it was the right kind of bark after all," he said.